For my niece, Sanaa — RPW

For my cousins: Makoto, Takashi, Sayaka, Rin, Haruka, Patrice, Claire and Veronique — MS

Text copyright © 2020 by Robert Paul Weston
Illustrations copyright © 2020 by Misa Saburi

Tundra Books, an imprint of Penguin Random House Canada Young Readers,
a Penguin Random House Company

Library and Archives Canada Cataloguing in Publication

Title: Natsumi's song of summer / Robert Paul Weston ; illustrated by Misa Saburi.
Names: Weston, Robert Paul, author. | Saburi, Misa, illustrator.
Identifiers: Canadiana (print) 20190122625 | Canadiana (ebook) 20190123087 | ISBN 9780735265417 (hardcover) | ISBN 9780735265424 (EPUB)
Classification: LCC PS8645.E87 N38 2020 | DDC jC813/.6—dc23

Published simultaneously in the United States of America by Tundra Books of Northern New York, an imprint of Penguin Random House Canada Young Readers, a Penguin Random House Company

Library of Congress Control Number: 2019942221

Edited by Lynne Missen
Designed by Rachel Cooper
The artwork in this book was rendered in Photoshop.
The text was set in Horley Old Style.

Printed and bound in China

www.penguinrandomhouse.ca

1 2 3 4 5   24 23 22 21 20

Natsumi's Song of Summer

Robert Paul Weston

Misa Saburi

tundra

In lotus season
with petals on every pond
Natsumi was born.

That was how she got her name.
It means "the sea in summer."

She loved everything
about summertime: swimming,
running on soft grass,

the sun, the heat, the cool bursts
of plum rain, heavy and sweet.

But what she loved most
were summer's insects, gleaming,
crawling, fluttering . . .

With their songs and bright bodies
the air itself came to life!

There were butterflies
with their striped and spotted wings,
and the sudden sparks

of fireflies, and honeybees
fizzing flower to flower.

There were mantises,
long green monks, always praying,
and the speckled gems

of ladybirds, red rubies
upon deep blue bellflowers.

But nothing could beat
the chirrup of cicadas!
Her mother would say,

"Summer has not yet begun
until their song fills the air."

On hot Saturdays
Natsumi and her parents
went searching for them.

With soft nets on bamboo poles
they reached up, rustling them free.

Natsumi sometimes
let one crawl along her arm.
It tickled her skin

while its body drummed and chirped.
Then, wings flitting, it was gone.

Natsumi's birthday
would soon arrive, and this year
it would be special.

Someone would come to visit
from the far side of the sea.

It was her cousin,
a girl named Jill, but someone
who was a stranger.

Although they were related
the two girls had never met.

But now, this summer,
Jill and her parents at last
had planned a visit.

Natsumi was excited
but she was also nervous.

What would Jill be like?
What would they have in common?
Would they become friends?

Or perhaps they would quarrel?
There was no way of knowing.

At the huge airport
Natsumi saw her cousin
weaving through the crowds,

grinning and anxious, her eyes
bright with curiosity.

"Show me everything!"
Jill chimed, her voice like a bell.
"Everything there is!"

"*Everything?*" asked Natsumi.
Where would she even begin?

Perhaps at the beach,
where hot sand powdered their toes,
and cool on their tongues

mouthfuls of watermelon
turned their lips a rosy pink.

Or at the *obon*
festival, where together
they danced, hands waving

giving thanks to the spirits
of their countless ancestors.

Or by the river
their faces tipped to the stars
watching the fireworks

as they bloomed in the night sky
all the colors of summer.

Everywhere they went
Jill squinted into the trees
listening closely

and asking the same question,
"What is all that bizz-buzzing?"

Jill came from a place
where there were few cicadas.
She had never seen

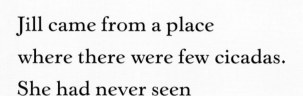

their large eyes and glossy wings
or heard their chittering hum.

Natsumi wanted
to show them to her cousin
but she was worried.

Insects frightened some people.
What if Jill was frightened, too?

Natsumi's birthday
arrived with a bright blue sky
but Jill still squinted

into the treetop shadows
where hidden cicadas thrummed.

"I'll show them to you,"
Natsumi said. She scampered
into the cool house

and returned with two soft nets
each atop a bamboo pole.

They swept the branches
and a pair of cicadas
looped down to meet them.

Would Jill be scared? Would she scream?
No. She crouched low, eyes sparkling.

"They're born underground," Natsumi explained. "For years they wait in darkness.

But then, when they're old enough they climb out to meet their friends."

"Just like us," said Jill.
"Waiting and waiting, and now
we've finally met!"

Natsumi smiled. She and Jill
were truly two of a kind.

They quietly watched
the two crawling cicadas
as their bodies drummed —

Miiin-min! Miiin-min! Min-min-min!
Then, wings *flitting*, they were gone.

In the afternoon
they drew pictures together.
Natsumi's drawing

was of the two cicadas
but Jill sketched out something else . . .

Elegant green wings
with two black-and-yellow spots
like half-winking eyes.

"What is it?" asked Natsumi.
"I've never seen one before."

"It's a luna moth,"
said Jill. "I think you'll see one
when you visit me."

Natsumi nodded, her eyes
bright with curiosity.

She knew tomorrow
Jill would fly home, but for now
they sat side by side

and listened, as the warm sky
filled with the song of summer.

Tanka

This story was written in a series of tanka poems. A tanka is a traditional Japanese poem with five lines and thirty-one syllables. The first three lines follow the same pattern as a haiku (5-7-5), but a tanka has two additional lines, each with seven syllables, for example:

Natsumi's story
was written in a series
of tanka poems.

If you enjoyed it, perhaps
you could write some of your own.

In Japan, cicadas are a symbol of summertime. They have large eyes, translucent wings and spend most of their lifespan underground — some for as long as seventeen years! It is only in the last week or two of their lives that they grow wings and emerge into the sunshine.

During these brief last days, male cicadas sing, using an organ in their abdomens called a tymbal. The sound attracts females so they can mate and reproduce.

The largest cicadas make sounds reaching ninety decibels, nearly as loud as a lawnmower!

For generations, Japanese poets have mimicked in words the sound of cicadas, giving each of the common species a sound of its own:

The evening cicada (*Tanna japonensis*)
Kana-kana-kana!

The min-min cicada (*Hyalessa maculaticollis*)
Miiiin! Min-min-min!

The large brown cicada (*Graptopsaltria nigrofuscata*)
Jii-jii! Jii-jii!

The kuma cicada (*Cryptotympana facialis*)
Shyaaa! Shyaaa!

Walker's cicada (*Meimuna opalifera*)
Tsuku-tsukoshi! Tsuku-tsukoshi!

The Kempfer cicada (*Platypleura kaempferi*)
Nii-nii! Nii-nii!

Have you ever heard an insect singing? What do you think it sounds like?